Rough and Tough

T-Bone

by Annie Streit

DORRANCE
PUBLISHING CO
EST. 1920
PITTSBURGH, PENNSYLVANIA 15238

Dorrance Publishing Co
585 Alpha Drive
Pittsburgh, PA 15238
Visit our website at *www.dorrancebookstore.com*

ISBN: 978-1-4809-9026-5

eISBN: 978-1-4809-9010-4

This is dedicated to you, Robbie.

Thank you for filling my life and the life of so many others with unconditional love, laughter, and kindness.

Love, Aunt Nin

This is a story about T-Bone; he has an important lesson for you.

He once thought that being mean was the cool thing to do.

T-Bone is a bulldog, and he is not very tall.

He has a round nubby tail and rather large paws.

His hair is all white with a tan patch around one eye,

and even though he is short, his chest is quite wide.

He has a wrinkly face and small floppy ears,

and whenever there are noises, he tilts his head, so he can hear.

His crooked teeth can make him look so mean,

and some would even say he is the scariest dog they have ever seen!

He was called rough and tough because he was bossy and rude.

He made fun of others, and he had a bad attitude.

T-Bone was known as a bully, and he thought that was cool.

He did not like to listen or follow the rules.

He picked on other dogs that were much smaller than him.

He liked to scare them with his bark... again... and again...

Being a bully was the only thing T-Bone knew how to do.

He didn't know love, and he used to get teased all the time too.

T-Bone wanted to make friends, but he didn't know how.

Dogs always ran away from him because of his snarl and scowl.

At the end of the day, he would walk home alone.

His only company was a chewed up dog bone.

Then, one day T-Bone ran into a boy that was much

bigger than him.

His name was Robbie, and he was walking with a grin.

Robbie was special because his heart was full of so much love.

He knew no strangers, and he would always greet

them with a hug.

Robbie was born different, with a gift that is so special and rare.

He does not believe in hate, and he treats everyone with so much care.

His eyes will brighten your day because they are the bluest of blues.

He has feelings, just like you and me, and he likes doing things that all kids do.

When he laughs, it sounds like it comes all the way from his belly.

He loves dogs, the beach, and peanut butter and jelly!

T-Bone would bark at Robbie and try to scare him away,

but Robbie never ran because he just wanted to play.

He would pat his legs with excitement and say, "C'mere boy!"

And he would bring T-Bone treats and loud squeaky toys.

You see, Robbie was teaching T-Bone the importance of friends,

and T-Bone started to understand that his bullying

must come to an end.

Every day, Robbie would visit, and T-Bone started to

feel something in his heart.

It was a feeling of love, and he began to hate being apart.

Now, T-Bone cannot wait to see Robbie every day after school.

His frown has turned into a smile... but he still has some drool.

T-Bone runs around in circles like he is a puppy again!

He is so sorry for being mean, and now, he just wants

to make friends.

T-Bone learned to apologize for the mean things he once did.

Robbie helped to show him how others can forgive.

So, always remember: if you mess up, you can learn

from your mistakes.

You have to be brave and open your heart because you

have what it takes!

T-Bone does not scare the other dogs, and he is no longer alone.

Robbie taught him that bullying is not the right way to go.

T-Bone sleeps better at night

because he knows tomorrow will be great,

and his dreams are full of how many new friends he can make.

Robbie and T-Bone have shown us how to open our

hearts and give as much love as we can,

because you never know who can become your best friend!

This world needs you to spread more love, cheer, and laughter,

and never forget that we all deserve friendships

and happily-ever-afters!

CPSIA information can be obtained
at www.ICGtesting.com
Printed in the USA
BVHW062230211019
561708BV00003B/4/P